TRISTINA BROCKWAY

On Your Knees

A FORBIDDEN PRIEST ROMANCE

TRISTINA BROCKWAY

For all the good girls going to hell.
See you there bitches!

Content Warning

On Your Knees is a dark, taboo, age gap, small town, priest romance with various tropes.

Age Gap (30+ years), Small Town, Dual POV, Priest, Virgin FMC, Family Secrets, Daddy Kink, Taboo, Forbidden Romance.

Contents

1. Bella — 1
2. Elijah — 7
3. Bella — 13
4. Elijah — 19
5. Bella — 25
6. Elijah — 31
7. Bella — 37
8. Elijah — 43
9. Bella — 51
10. Elijah — 57
11. Bella — 65
12. Elijah — 71
13. Bella — 75
14. Elijah — 81
15. Bella — 87
16. Elijah — 91
Epilogue — 97

Acknowledgments — 99
About the Author — 101
Also by Tristina Brockway — 103

CHAPTER 1
Bella

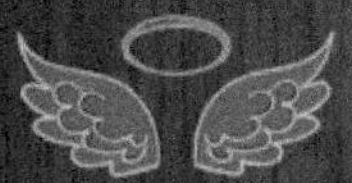

I sit in the hard wooden pew surrounded by members of the congregation, each looks enraptured in the words flowing from the pulpit.

Some of the flock are struck by the teachings coming from our holy leader, while others try their best to hide their sins they so desperately wish no one could see with hopes of washing them away and finding eternal salvation in the ever-lasting light of the lord.

We listen to the Sunday morning sermon as Father Elijah drones on about the sanctity of a holy union and what awaits those who disregard god and his many words of warning that the marriage bed should be undefiled.

I've always tried my best to steer clear of the immoral men who freely spill lies from their deceitful tongues, much like the serpent in the Garden of Eden, in hopes of bedding any young woman that should cross their path.

I've managed to stay pure for the first seventeen years of my life, but tomorrow is my eighteenth birthday and I can't help but let my eyes roam and my imagination run wild as I embrace the warm honeyed tone of his voice.

Father Elijah has salt and pepper hair and exudes an air of

wisdom and experience. He's dressed in a black button up shirt with a white collar, standard for a man of the cloth, and slacks that complements his build. As he stands at the pulpit during the Sunday service, his presence commands attention. And like the dutiful young woman that I am, I oblige.

Mother dressed me today, as she does every Sunday. It's been this way ever since my father left when I was a little girl. Gran said mother has to look pretty on the outside because if any man ever saw what existed on the inside, they would run far away, too. Just like father did.

They really do think so little of me. Mother may try to keep me in the dark about most things, but much to her dismay, people talk. And this town has been talking for years about her and my father's failed attempt at a happy life.

What I've heard around town is nothing short of a rumor mill if I've ever heard one. Some say father left to be with his new family. Some say he left to be with his old family that he had before mother and I. And some even go so far as to say he hasn't left this town at all and is most certainly six feet deep in the garden out back.

Now wouldn't that be a sight.

I start to giggle but quickly reign it in and stumble out a cough to cover my amusement instead. For a split second I could have sworn Father Elijah had a hint of amusement in his eyes.

I grind my teeth together as I feel the skin of my thigh pinch between two talons attached to none other than my doting mother. Ever the god fearing woman she turned out to be.

My leg feels like it's been stung by a wasp, but this tends to happen most Sunday's so it's nothing I'm not already use to. It's still annoying none the less.

She needs to be seen as the perfect woman with the perfect daughter and the perfect home.

Perfect. Perfect. Perfect.

Sometimes I just wish she would shut up for good. The incessant nagging is enough to drive any man away. Especially any that might have been worth keeping. If any chose to stay, I decided they weren't worth much to begin with because who in their right mind would put up with *her*, of all people?

I hurry to bow my head for prayer, as I notice that's what's next on the bulletin that I eagerly accepted when we entered the church this morning.

Whatever is on the schedule helps set the tone for the remainder of the hour.

I just love when someone gets baptized. While I wish it were because Jesus found his way into a member of our congregations heart, it's mostly because Father Elijah walks out of the pool looking like God himself after he performs his duties, causing his dress shirt and slacks to stick directly to his muscular chest, biceps. And thighs.

I quickly say a little prayer for myself, hoping the lord will help me with my perverse thoughts, while everyone else continues with the prayer that's spoken every Sunday like clockwork.

A chorus of *amen* breaks out around the sanctuary as the service comes to a close, and the sound of low chatter and gossip spreads throughout the room. Each family discussing their plans for what or where to have lunch with their family this afternoon.

I'm once again dragged behind mother as we make our way to the church doors to stand in line and say our good-byes to Father Elijah.

I feel the heat set in on my face and neck as we reach the front of the line. I'm not sure why today feels different. Father Elijah has been in our lives for years, always coming by to council my mother in her faith. She takes advantage of his position in the church to fill the role my biological father should have been playing in my life.

Maybe it's because I'm certain I was caught with my hand in the cookie jar, so to speak, that today feels different. Perhaps more like perusing his assets when I should have been singing the hymn along with everyone else.

I run my hands down my powder blue cotton dress that sits just above my knees and ever so slightly clings to my small frame to make sure it's not creased from sitting for so long, but also to ensure the clammy feeling in my palms is long gone by the time he shakes my hand.

Almost there. Only a few more steps.

CHAPTER 2
Elijah

I say a quick prayer to help me get through the next round of farewells as Mrs. Thornfield approaches the door. The only thing that makes her worth putting up with is the angel trailing behind her wearing a shiny halo. I swear that girl glows like she's an ethereal being not made to walk this earth.

I'm not sure what god had in mind when he created her, but I doubt it was for me to drop to my knees and worship at her alter. It's a shame, really.

I can only imagine how divine she would taste.

I do my best to push those sinful thoughts to the back of my mind and clear my throat, reaching my hand out to shake the scorned older woman's. It feels as if I have to pry my fingers out of her grip as I pull away.

I hurry to shake her daughters hand in hopes that her mother won't grab mine again.

Her daughter, Isabella, is a stark contrast to her mother. She has the same beauty, except Isabella is just *more*. More *everything*. Her eyes hold a warmth and kindness that Mrs. Thornfield lacks.

As I shake Isabella's hand, I can't help but notice the

gentle touch and genuine smile that graces her lips. It's a welcome relief to have a momentary reprieve from the tension that always seems to accompany Mrs. Thornfield's presence.

"Good to see you, Isabella." I say as I hold her hand in mine.

"Just Bella. Good to see you, too, Father Elijah." She shyly whispers her reply. I enjoy her response every time I call her by her full given name each time we meet, which is quite often.

Her rosy red cheeks and flushed neck and chest tell me that she's just as affected by our exchange as I am. The only difference is I've had decades of practice at hiding my earthly desires. She's had mere years. If she thinks she hides her desire, she's sorely mistaken.

She flutters her lashes and looks up to meet my eyes and I'm taken aback once again by the light blue orbs that greet my dark blue ones. I catch a glimpse of a mischievous sparkle in Bella's eyes.

It's as if she knows the effect her mother has on people and finds amusement in it. I can't help but be drawn to her playful nature, finding solace in the fact that there is more to her than meets the eye.

But as quickly as the moment of respite arrives, it fades away. Mrs. Thornfield clears her throat, reminding us all of her presence. She pulls Bella away, leaving me standing there, feeling a mix of disappointment and longing. It's a familiar feeling, one that has become all too common in my interactions with the Thornfield family throughout the years.

I watch as they disappear through the door, the angelic glow of Bella's presence fading with each step. I can't help but wonder what it would be like to have her by my side, to experience her light and warmth on a daily basis instead of once or twice a week. But reality sets in, reminding me of the vast divide between us. My position in the church, not to mention the age difference. The congregation would be in an uproar.

I take a deep breath, trying to shake off the lingering thoughts and emotions. It's time to focus on the task at hand, to navigate the sea of farewells and polite conversations that lie ahead. But deep down, I can't help but hope that one day I'll have the chance to taste the divine sweetness that Bella embodies.

I STAND AT THE PODIUM GIVING A SERMON TO THE CONGREGATION and look up to see Bella sitting in the front pew next to her mother. Despite her mothers presence, or perhaps in spite of it, Bella slowly inches her dress up her thighs and scoots down a little in her seat, spreading her legs slightly apart, giving me a preview of what I want so badly to touch and taste.

I give her a look and she knows what to do. Sliding to the floor, everyone begins to look at her as she crawls towards me and up the five steps to the alter. I watch her breasts gently sway as she makes her way towards me.

Once she reaches her destination directly in front of me, kneeling at my feet, she doesn't stop as she undoes my pants and frees my cock from the restraint of the fabric.

I stop speaking for only a moment to lean down and give her further instructions.

I whisper in her ear, "Be a good girl and make daddy come."

She licks the tip of my cock. Tasting the pre-cum on her tongue, she hums in approval. Swirling her tongue around the head and then slowly licks up and down each side of my shaft, she makes her way down and back up one side and then moves to the other, stopping to lick and slowly suck my heavy balls into that sweet but sinful mouth of hers.

Once she lifts back up she places the head of my dick in her mouth and sucks as hard as she can. With a swiftness she opens her throat and slams her head against my pelvis shoving my length down the back of her throat and holds it, then swallows. I feel her throat constrict around me. Once her eyes start to water she pulls herself back slowly, continuing to suck leisurely along the way.

She brings a hand up to follow her mouth and as she drags her lips off of me, she twists her head and hands in opposite directions and goes back down on me creating an unbelievable sensation that nearly has me wanting to shoot my load down her throat right then and there, but I wait.

Bella goes on to work my cock like she's a seasoned professional and not the barely legal eighteen year old that she now is.

The rhythm continues to build as everyone else watches on, but bows their heads to pray as I lead us in worship.

"Dear heavenly father…" I say with a rasp.

I BOLT UP IN THE MIDDLE OF MY BED FROM THE MOST INTENSE dream I've had in a good long while. I'm covered in sweat and breathing heavily.

I reach to pull the sheets back over me since I've kicked the majority of the covers off of the bed from my tossing and turning, and can't help but notice my cock is standing at full attention, hard as a rock.

"*Fuck.*" I whisper to myself.

I reach down and squeeze my length trying to silently command it to go back to sleep, but it does the opposite. Somehow, hardening even more.

Visions from my dreams begin to swirl in my mind and I find I have no more restraint left in me tonight.

I lay back in the bed and stroke my cock at a furious pace, imagining the scene from my dreams.

"Fuck!" I yell as I jump up, head for the bathroom, and get into the shower, blasting cold water over my entire body and my cum all over the shower wall.

"It was just a dream." I murmur to myself as I take in a deep breath and sigh in both disappointment and relief.

For now.

CHAPTER 3

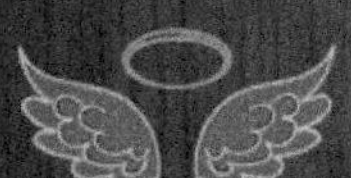

T oday is my eighteenth birthday. I've been impatiently waiting for this day ever since I learned all of the benefits that come with it in the eyes of the law.

You would think I would be most excited to leave my mother behind, moving out of Thornfield Manor to have a life of my own now that I was of age. But I've accepted that this is something I won't be able to do right away.

Not with mother suffocating me every second of every day.

I could legally buy cigarettes should I ever have the desire to die a slow and painful death brought on by a disease that spreads through my lungs causing me to suffocate day in and day out until the very end.

No thank you.

Or serve in the military should I desire to enlist. But I'm barely surviving my mother. I can't even imagine how I would make it through a deployment.

Not happening.

The biggest perk of this new year in the life of Bella Thornfield is without a doubt the fact that I can now legally fornicate with any man I desire.

The biggest downfall is that there's no way on god's green earth the only man I desire would ever want me in the way I want him. Especially when mother is staring at him across the dinner table like he's her *last supper*.

"Amen," Father Elijah says to end the blessing of the food before we eat.

"This looks delicious. Thank you, Mrs. Thornfield."

I can't help but snort in amusement as Father Elijah thanks mother for the meal we're about to consume, as if she ever sets foot in the kitchen unless it's to order the people around who actually *do* prepare the food we enjoy.

"It's my pleasure, Father Elijah." She coos as she reaches over giving my thigh a pinch while once again deeply digging her fingernails into my skin. I wouldn't be surprised if she broke the skin, drawing blood yet again.

I continue to keep my gaze lowered to the food on my plate, holding in a whimper, while working diligently to contain the tears filling my eyes.

I refuse to let this woman see me cry, knowing it would bring her nothing but joy to hear my pain. She'll have to settle for watching me suffer in silence instead. Unfortunately for me, I'm pretty sure she enjoys that almost as much.

She's been trying for years to break me, and she has many times. But she's yet to break me in front of the man in front of us and I intend to keep it that way.

I refuse to give her the satisfaction of knowing how much she truly affects me. I take a deep breath, trying to steady myself, and force a smile as I respond, "Yes, thank you, mother. It looks absolutely delicious."

Father Elijah shoots me a concerned glance, but I quickly divert my gaze, not wanting him to get involved in this twisted dynamic. He's always been oblivious to Mother's true nature, blinded by her charm and beauty. But I know the truth, and I've learned to navigate this treacherous household on my own.

As I take a bite of the food, I can't help but notice the exquisite flavors that dance on my tongue. The chef, who remains hidden behind the kitchen doors, is the true artist behind these culinary masterpieces. I silently thank them for their skill and dedication, knowing that they are the ones who truly deserve the praise.

Mother, on the other hand, revels in the attention and adoration she receives for simply being the lady of the house. She thrives on the power she holds over everyone, especially me. But I refuse to let her break me. I will endure her cruelty and manipulation, biding my time until I can escape this suffocating existence.

With each passing day, I grow stronger, more determined to forge my own path. I dream of a life where I am free from Mother's clutches, where I can pursue my own passions and surround myself with people who genuinely care for me. Until then, I will play the part of the obedient daughter, hiding my true emotions behind a mask of obedience.

As the dinner conversation continues, I remain silent, observing the interactions between Father Elijah and mother. I see through their charade, and it only fuels my determination to escape this toxic environment.

One day, I will break free from my mothers control. And when that day comes, I will leave behind the darkness of this household and step into the light of my own destiny. Until then, I will endure, and find solace in the small moments of defiance that keep my spirit alive.

After we finish our meal, mother dismisses me with the expectation that I'll go straight to my room and adhere to my nightly routine of bathing, brushing my teeth and hair, slipping into my nightgown, and following the nightly skin regimen she's ordered me to adhere to for as long as I can remember. This is followed by reading my bible and then kneeling at my bedside to say my bedtime prayers before slipping into dreamland, only to wake up and do it all over again the next day.

I STARTLE AWAKE TO THE SOUND OF A THUMP, UNSURE OF HOW long I've been asleep. I lay in bed for a few minutes listening for the sounds to see if it was my imagination running wild while I slumbered and hear the sound a few more times.

Unable to determine what or where the sound is coming from I get out of bed and slip from my room to get a glass of water and investigate the strange noise.

As I walk down the hall I hear muffled voices coming from the wing opposite mine. Sounds easily echo through our quiet, empty house in the dead of night.

I tiptoe down the hall. The closer I get to my mothers room, the more distinguishable the voices become.

"Oh god!" I hear my mother's voice and assume she is upset and seeking guidance from the lord through prayer. But that's followed closely by a thumping noise and then the slapping begins.

"Take it." I hear a male voice growl.

It suddenly hits me that I'm baring witness to my mother sinning more than I ever have in my life. Yet, she treats me like the biggest sinner she's ever known.

I can't help but be drawn to her bedroom door. I'm dying to see who she's caught and spun in her web of deceit. I slowly make my way to the opening and peek through where the door has been left ajar just enough to get an eye full of betrayal.

I feel as though my eyes should be soaked in holy water after bearing witness to the acts taking place between Father

Elijah and my mother. But the truth is I can't blame either of them.

There are many reasons why my crush on the father could never be anything more than just that. A simple crush. He's a priest, which now that I see what's in front of me really doesn't have that much weight to it right now. However, the age difference between us is as vast as the Grand Canyon.

It's now my birthday, so my eighteen years compared to Father Elijah's fifty-two on this earth, really leaves no comparison. I'm young, inexperienced. Why would he want me when he can have someone like my mother, who is obviously more suited to the role of a whore.

But I can't seem to remove my eyes from the nightmare currently unfolding before my very eyes, only mere feet away from where I stand.

I've somehow managed to tune my mother out completely and take in the slight smirk pulling at the corner of Father Elijah's mouth.

My eyes dart to his and I quickly realize my mistake. His eyes were already locked on mine when I met his gaze.

CHAPTER 4
Elijah

I watch the little intruder dart away from the door. The look of curiosity and intrigue on her face as she stood there is enough to make me find my release. *Finally.*

Regina fakes another orgasm. Why, I'm not sure. I already gave her a couple and it wasn't even my intension to do so. I could care less if she gets anything out of this arrangement. But it usually takes me so long to get there that she's bound to have one or two along the way.

We've had this arrangement for years now. She keeps my secret and I keep hers. But I rarely give in to her advances. However, the dream I had of Bella the other night has left my mind shattered into pieces and up is hard to distinguish from down right now. I needed something to take the edge off and distract me from her tempting daughter.

I back up and tuck my length back into my slacks. No need to get completely undressed. I never allow foreplay. I fear that would give Regina Thornfield too much hope and ammunition should she decide to play a card or two. No idea what game it would be but I've known her long enough to know that manipulation is the name of her game and she plays it well.

"Darling, won't you stay?" She desperately whines as I gather my things and head for the door.

I pause for a moment, my hand on the doorknob. The desperation in her voice is palpable, but I know better than to give in to her pleas. If I give an inch she'll take a mile. I turn to face her, my expression firm and resolute.

"Regina, we've been down this road before," I say, my voice steady. "It's a dangerous game, one that I refuse to play with you. You know this."

Her eyes narrow, a flicker of anger crossing her features before she quickly masks it with a seductive smile. "But Elijah, we've had our arrangement for years. You can't deny that there's something between us."

I shake my head, "What we have is nothing more than a twisted illusion, Regina. We use each other. That's all it's ever been and all it will ever be. But it's time we face the truth and move on." She's been pressing her luck lately and with the look on her face I can tell she's hoping for much more than I will ever give. I can barely stand the woman as it is.

She takes a step closer, her voice dropping to a low, sultry whisper. "You can't deny the passion we share, Elijah. It's intoxicating, undeniable."

I grit my teeth and take a deep breath to try and sooth my anger. This is why I never should have agreed to this all those years ago.

"You were a convenience. Nothing more. I made it very clear from the beginning." I remind her.

Her eyes flash with a mix of frustration and desperation. "You're making a mistake, Elijah. You'll regret walking away from me."

I meet her gaze, my voice filled with determination. "Our lives are intertwined enough as it is. It's time we end this arrangement and move on from it."

I depart from her room, closing the door behind me.

I may be entangled in a web of secrets and deceit, but I

refuse to play her games. I will find a way to untangle myself from this twisted existence, one way or another.

I head for the stairs but find myself passing them by to see what Bella's up to and if she returned to her room after catching her mother and I together.

Sounds of frustration are coming from behind the door. I slowly turn the knob and peek inside to find Bella sitting in front of a full length mirror. *Naked*.

Her legs are spread apart with her newly turned eighteen year old pussy reflecting back at her in the mirror. It's obvious she's never groomed herself with the hair covering her intimate area. But it's not too bad. She could trim if she'd like. I personally would prefer to see her bare.

I watch as she flattens her hand, cupping herself between the legs, and attempts to what looks like a mixture of squeezing and rubbing the whole area at once and can't help the grin that spreads across my face. I hold in the chuckle that's dying to be let free.

I can only assume the poor girl is trying to masturbate, and by the repeated grunts of frustration, not pleasure, coming from her lips, no one has ever taught her how to do so.

A mix of guilt and desire swirls within me, battling for dominance. I know I shouldn't be here, shouldn't be invading her privacy like this, but curiosity and a twisted sense of longing compel me to stay.

Bella's eyes widen in shock as she catches sight of me in the reflection of the mirror. She quickly covers herself, a flush of embarrassment spreading across her cheeks. "Father Elijah! What are you doing here?" she stammers, her voice filled with a mixture of surprise and unease.

I step further into the room, my gaze locked with hers. "I apologize, Bella. I didn't mean to intrude. I was just... checking to see if you were okay," I stumble over my words, my mind racing to find a plausible excuse for my presence.

She crosses her arms over her chest, her eyes narrowing with suspicion. "Checking if I'm okay? By barging into my room unannounced?" Her tone is laced with a hint of anger, but also a flicker of curiosity.

I take a deep breath, trying to regain my composure. "I heard some noises, and I thought something might be wrong. I didn't mean to invade your privacy, Bella. Please forgive me."

I can't help but think of how ironic it is that she's playing this game with me after only moments ago I caught her watching me with wonder as I railed her mother.

She studies me for a moment, her expression softening slightly. "Fine, Father Elijah. Just... please, knock next time. I value my privacy."

I nod, "Of course, Bella. I promise it won't happen again."

As I turn to leave, a part of me wonders what would have happened if I walked even further into the room and continued to watch her. My smile appears to return, but I quickly push that thought aside, knowing that indulging in such fantasies would only lead to further destruction.

"Father Elijah?" She calls out a I begin to leave.

"Yes?" I ask.

She surprises me by slowly lowering her hands, revealing her perky young breasts to me once again. Her long blonde hair flows down either side caressing them. Her small pink nipples are puckered up with me eager to flick my tongue back and forth across the tightened little buds.

I can see the fear of rejection in her eyes clear as day.

"Would you show me how?" She whispers.

I feel a rush of eagerness and disbelief wash over me as I try to comprehend the situation unfolding before my eyes. This young woman, who had sought my guidance and solace, was now standing before me with a request that crossed boundaries I never anticipated.

My mind races, searching for the right words to respond,

but all I can manage is a stammered, "I... I'm sorry, but that's not appropriate. I am here to offer spiritual guidance, not to engage in such intimate matters."

I know as soon as I speak the words that I'm full of shit. She took me by surprise. Today's her eighteenth birthday and I've been counting down the days.

Her expression shifts from fear to disappointment, and I can sense the vulnerability in her voice as she softly pleads, "Please, Father Elijah, I don't know who else to turn to. I trust you, and I need your help."

I watch as her eyes fill up with tears. My heart aches for her, recognizing the pain and confusion she must be experiencing. But as a man of faith, I am bound by my vows and the moral code that guides my actions. Then again, my soul is already marked for hell so fuck morality. If I'm going to hell it might as well be worth the ride.

CHAPTER 5
Bella

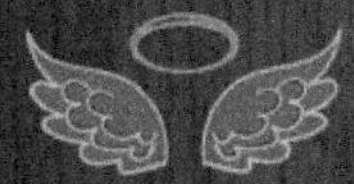

"Tell me what you need," Father Elijah demands. I can't help but let my relief and happiness show as I exhale my long held breath and return his beautiful smile.

"I've never…never touched myself before." I blurt out so fast it's as if the words were burning my tongue. "Truth is, I'm not really sure what I'm doing."

I can see the amusement dancing in his eyes and can only hope he doesn't make fun of me. If catching him with my mother is any indication, he's clearly into older women. Not young ones, like myself.

"And what would you like me to do for you Bella?" He quietly asks as he continues his path towards me.

"I…I was hoping you would show me how to…how to make myself feel good." I reply.

He quietly growls before attempting to cover the noise by rubbing his hand over his mouth.

"Come here. Turn around." He orders while holding out his hand for me to take. I do as he says, taking his hand and turning around to face the full length mirror.

He wraps his arms around my waist, resting his chin on my shoulder, while using his right hand to guide mine between my legs. I suck in a sharp breath as his touch sends a jolt of electricity through my body. My heart races, and I can feel the heat rising to my cheeks. The intensity of the moment is overwhelming, and I can't help but tremble in his embrace.

His voice, low and husky, whispers in my ear, "Feel how much power you have over me." His words send shivers down my spine, and I can't deny the desire that courses through my veins as he presses his length against me from behind. With his guidance, my fingers explore the warmth between my legs, finding the sensitive bundle of nerves within seconds.

Every touch, every caress, ignites a fire within me, and I can't help but let out a soft moan. The sound is swallowed by the room, but it only fuels his hunger. His grip tightens around my waist, his breath hot against my skin, as he watches me in the mirror.

He guides my fingers to my opening and presses them inside just enough for me to coat them in the warm slickness leaking from inside me. Then moves my fingers back to the sensitive nub higher up.

As our hands move in sync, the mirror becomes a witness to my pleasure, and I can feel myself teetering on the precipice of ecstasy.

But just as the intensity reaches its peak, he releases his grip and steps back, leaving me breathless and wanting. His eyes meet mine in the mirror, a mischievous glint dancing within them. "Keep going," he whispers.

I bite my lip, a mixture of frustration and anticipation coursing through me. I continue to rub back and forth, picking up speed. My breath coming in quick shallow pants.

"Please." I beg Father Elijah even though I have no idea what I'm begging for. But it feels like something only he can give me.

A smile spreads across his lips as if he's pleased at the turn of events. He takes a small step forward and once again I feel his left hand land on my left hip and grip tight.

"Be a good girl and come for daddy." He whispers into my ear and that's all it takes for me to suddenly see stars dancing. Bursts of light pulsing behind my eyelids keeping rhythm with the pulsating of my core.

I hear a low growl as I look up and lock eyes once again in the mirror with Father Elijah before feeling a splash of warmth land in rivulets across my behind, one, two, three times.

I've heard of a man's seed but have never seen it, and most certainly have never felt it before now. Curiosity wins out and I reach behind me running my fingers through the warmth and bring it in front of me to see with my own eyes.

I smear it back and forth between my fingers, then dart out my tongue for a taste.

I pause for a moment, my fingers still glistening with his essence, as a mix of shock and arousal washes over me. The taste is foreign yet strangely enticing.

With a hunger that surprises even myself, I bring my fingers to my lips once again, savoring the taste of Father Elijah's seed. The salty sweetness lingers on my tongue, and I find myself craving more. It's a moment of surrender, of giving in to the depths of my desires, as I clean up every last drop, relishing in the intimacy of this act.

Father Elijah's low growl of approval sends shivers down my spine.

"Good girl." He praises.

I hear the sound of his pants being zipped. He gives me a wink in the mirror and then leaves my room as quietly as he entered it.

A few minutes later I realize I'm still standing in the middle of my room with no clothes on contemplating if this was real or not.

Did Father Elijah just help me masturbate for the first time? Do I have the taste of his seed on my tongue? Did he really call himself my daddy and refer to me as his good girl? I'm pretty sure he did. *And I want more.*

I SPENT MOST OF THE NIGHT TOSSING AND TURNING IN BED, unable to let my mind settle. I still can't believe everything that happened last night.

I desperately try to push aside the haunting image of Father Elijah in the same room as my mother, being intimate. The mere thought of it sickens me, leaving a deep, gnawing knot of dread in the pit of my stomach.

In an attempt to maintain my sanity, I focus solely on what transpired after I retreated to my own room and he unexpectedly entered, agreeing to help me. I assumed his instruction would be the highlight of the lesson. Fortunately for me, he took it to a whole new level.

I don't know if he meant to show interest in me, or even me specifically, but now all I'm craving is him, even more than I thought possible.

It's as I have these thoughts that I decide right then and there that I want to learn more. I want him to teach me.

I want to know how to please a man, and not just any man, but him. Maybe if I show Father Elijah what I'm capable of he'll crave me as much as I crave him.

As these thoughts consume me, I feel a surge of determination coursing through my veins. With a newfound sense of purpose, I make a decision. I will seek out Father Elijah.

The thought of being rejected or worse, judged, sends a shiver down my spine. Yet, the burning desire within me refuses to be silenced.

I begin to devise a plan, carefully crafting my words and actions to entice Father Elijah. I will show him that I am willing to explore anything. I will prove to him that I am worthy of his attention and that I'm willing to let him mold me into whatever pleases him.

CHAPTER 6
Elijah

I sit in the confessional and listen to members of the congregation confess their sins. I often can't believe the things people actually have the nerve to confess.

Typically confessionals are made to be anonymous, but this is a small town. I find it hard to believe that Bradley Wallace honestly thinks I won't know it's him confessing to cheating on his wife with her sister. Or that Sandra May doesn't realize I can tell it's her confessing to sleeping with her cousin.

The things people think they can get away with by simply confessing their sins. Though I suppose that's pretty on point with how it's supposed to work. But I'm the last one to throw stones. Glass houses and all that.

I hear someone enter the confessional and know right away who is on the other side. I would recognize that scent anywhere. The combination of vanilla and sugar cookies. A fitting combination for my tempting little halo.

One would think she's innocent and she is in all the obvious ways. But her curiosity will be my undoing.

"Forgive me, father, for I have sinned. It's been twenty days since my last confession." Bella confesses.

"What troubles bring you here today?" I reply while trying to keep the smile on my face from coming through in my words.

"I spent my night tossing and turning, unable to sleep, for thoughts of lust and desire kept me awake and in thought. I just keep visualizing myself with a man of the cloth touching me in the most intimate ways. "

My heart skips a beat as Bella's words hang in the air. The confession booth suddenly feels suffocating, the air heavy with the weight of her forbidden desires. I struggle to maintain my composure.

Taking a deep breath, I gather my thoughts and respond, my voice steady. "Bella, these impure thoughts that plague your mind are indeed sinful. It is natural for temptation to test our faith, but it is our duty to resist and seek forgiveness."

I know damn well I don't mean a word of what I'm saying.

Bella's continues. "Father, I have tried to suppress these thoughts, to banish them from my mind, but they persist. I fear that my curiosity will lead me astray, that I will succumb to temptation."

It is a delicate situation. "My child, it is crucial to remember that curiosity, in itself, is not a sin. However, it is how we act upon that curiosity that determines our righteousness. It is essential to redirect your thoughts towards virtuous pursuits, to seek solace in prayer and reflection."

Bella's voice wavers, her vulnerability seeping through her words. "But, Father, what if these desires consume me? What if I am unable to resist the temptation?"

I pause for a moment, contemplating the weight of her confession. It is a battle that many have faced, the struggle between the desires of the flesh and the purity of the soul. One I've been disregarding for years. "Bella, we are all flawed beings, prone to temptation. But it is through our faith and the strength of our convictions that we find redemption. Seek guidance from the Lord, for He will provide you with the strength to overcome these trials."

Silence envelops the confessional, the weight of Bella's confession lingering in the air. As a priest, it is my duty to guide and support those who seek forgiveness, even when I'm not adhering to my own advice.

"Ever since last night I feel the need to touch myself. It felt so good father. I've never felt anything like it."

"And how did it feel?" I say in a raspy voice before I even realize what it is I've said.

Shit.

I hear a sharp intake of breath through the lattice and a small whimper.

"It feels warm. Wet. So good every time I rub between my legs. Even now. your voice makes me want to rub faster." She whispers.

She's touching herself. My little halo had a taste of ecstasy and now it's a drug that her body will always crave.

I try to fight it. To fight my desire to walk around this inconvenient box that divides us and take her right here and now. But I can't.

So I do just that and pray that no one knows what's about to happen.

I walk into her side of the confessional and she gasps in shock, her dress pull up around her waist and her hand in her cute white cherry covered panties. But like a good girl she continues.

I prop both hands on the back of the room on either side of her head and lean down into her face with my lips almost touching hers.

"Is this what you want?" I whisper, and she nods her head yes. "Words," I reply.

"Yes." She says again while nodding her head again.

I kneel down before her and slide her panties down her legs removing them and stuffing them inside my pocket.

I lean down placing my head between her legs and inhale her glorious sweet yet musky scent. If it were up to me, this is the only air I would breath for eternity. I can't help but groan while gripping the outline of my cock through my pants.

I continue my forward momentum and quickly flick my tongue over her clit. I lock my gaze on her face to bear witness to every response she has to my touch.

I've seen a variety of cunts in my fifty-two years, but my halo's is by far the most gorgeous, enticing of them I've ever seen. Her mound sits high and tight, visible through her pink plump little lips that cozy up to each side.

I lift her legs, placing them over my shoulders to tilt her hips slightly higher so that I'm able to view the honeypot that awaits me.

She stares down at me with innocent doe eyes, panting, not knowing what she's in for. That single look is all it takes for my resolve to crumble in a matter of seconds.

I lean forward and swirl my tongue around her entrance, lapping up the pool of arousal that's calling to me.

My senses are overwhelmed by the intoxicating taste of her desire, fueling my own hunger. I nudge my tongue slightly inside her virgin pussy, testing to see how tight she might be in order to try my best not to minimize the pain when I take her for the first time. It won't be today, but it will be soon.

I slide my tongue up and suck gently on her bundle of nerves.

Then, with each flick of my tongue, I feel her body tremble, her grip on reality slipping away. I can sense her surrender, her vulnerability laid bare before me. I continue to tease and torment, alternating between gentle caresses and firm pressure, building the anticipation that hangs thick in the air.

"Oh god," Bella whimpers.

"Not god. Daddy. Say it my little halo. Tell me who your daddy is." I growl into her slit.

"You," She mewls. "You're my daddy."

"That's right. Now be a good girl and come for your daddy, baby."

I dive in and lap up her sweet juices and then move back up to her clit. Her hips begin to buck, a silent plea for more. I oblige, my mouth now fully enveloping her, my lips creating a seal that intensifies the sensations coursing through her.

I apply more pressure and flick my tongue back and forth quickly, pushing her to the edge, causing her to fall over. "Daddy!" She cries and her voice bounces off of the confessional walls. Shattering, her body convulsing with waves of pleasure, I drink in every drop of her essence, savoring the taste of her satisfaction.

Her tight entrance contracts over and over again, around nothing, begging to be filled. I hum as I suck and nibble on her clit once again guiding her through her release.

It doesn't take long until she reaches the other side. She continues to pant, trying to catch her breath. As she comes down from her euphoric high, I gently release her legs from my shoulders, allowing her to regain her composure.

Our eyes meet and I lean forward, pressing my lips to hers. She squeaks in surprise. I can tell this is her first kiss not only from her initial reaction but from the way she doesn't move her mouth at all, as if waiting for me to guide her.

I slide my tongue along her lips seeking permission and she opens in response. Our tongues intertwine in a sensual dance. I want to make sure she gets as much of her flavor in her mouth as I have in mine.

"See how good you taste? Daddy won't be able to get enough. You gonna be a good girl and let daddy eat it whenever he gets hungry?"

"Yes, daddy." She whispers in response to my request.

"Good girl."

I can only hope that we're still alone in the church and that I'm the only witness to our sinful confession.

CHAPTER 7
Bella

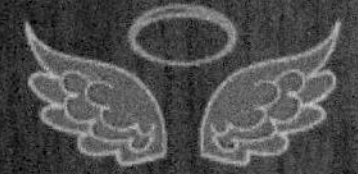

"I can't believe Mr. Addams isn't married. I mean seriously. How hot is he? And young, too!" Lindsey said excitedly.

We both tumbled into the grass by the pond. I rolled over into my back staring at the clouds in the sky.

"I don't know. He's not really my type." I said reluctantly.

"What do you mean? He's everyone's type!"

"Well, I don't know. Maybe young isn't everyone's preference."

Lindsey rolled over onto her stomach and smacked my arm with the back of her hand as she scoffed. "Isabella Thornfield! You tell me right now who this old man is that you obviously have the hots for!"

I couldn't help the nervous giggle that escaped me. I know I can trust Lindsey. We've been friends since we were little. If I told anyone about my forbidden crush, it would be her. She's loyal to a fault. She also attends our church. So I'm not sure if she would ever be able to look at Father Elijah the same again.

"Come on Bell! Tell meeeee…. Pretty please?"

I take a deep breath and try my best to prepare for whatever reaction I may get from her, be it good or bad.

I hesitated for a moment, contemplating whether or not to reveal my secret. Lindsey's curiosity was relentless, and I knew she wouldn't let it go until she had an answer. Taking a deep breath, I decided to confide in her, hoping she would understand.

"Okay, fine. But promise me you won't judge," I said, my voice barely above a whisper.

Lindsey's eyes widened with anticipation, her curiosity piqued. "I promise, Bella. You know I won't judge you. Now spill!"

I shifted uncomfortably, feeling a mix of embarrassment and excitement. "It's Father Elijah," I finally admitted, my cheeks flushing crimson.

Lindsey's jaw dropped, her eyes widening even further. "Father Elijah? Our priest? Are you serious?"

I nodded, unable to meet her gaze. "I know it sounds crazy, but there's something about him. His kindness, his wisdom, the way he carries himself. It's like he has this magnetic presence that draws me in."

Lindsey's expression softened, her initial shock giving way to understanding. "Bella, I get it. Sometimes, we can't control who we're attracted to. But he's a priest, and you know the rules."

I do know the rules, but she doesn't know he's already broke them. First with my mother. Now with me. So I go ahead and fill her in on everything that's happened the last few days.

" I mean, none of us are perfect, even if he is supposed to be a pillar of virtue." She says, trying to take the sting out of her previous response. But making us laugh, once again breaking the tension.

"So how was it?" Lindsey asks with an impish grin.

"Incredible." I quickly reply.

I couldn't help but let out a nervous giggle, grateful for Lindsey's attempt to lighten the heavy atmosphere. Her playful question caught me off guard, but I knew she was just trying to support me in her own unique way.

"Incredible doesn't even begin to describe it," I confessed, a blush creeping up my cheeks. "It was like nothing I've ever experienced before. The intensity, it was overwhelming."

Lindsey's eyes widened, a mix of curiosity and excitement dancing within them. "Tell me everything! I want all the juicy details."

I hesitated for a moment, unsure of how much I should reveal. But Lindsey's genuine enthusiasm and unwavering support reassured me. With a mischievous smile, I began recounting the passionate encounter, leaving no detail untouched.

Lindsey listened intently, her eyes sparkling with intrigue. "Wow, Bella. I can't even imagine. It sounds like a dream come true."

I nodded, a mix of emotions swirling within me. "It was, in a way. But it's also complicated, Lindsey. We haven't talked about it yet but I'm sure we both know the risks and the consequences of our actions. We can't ignore the reality of the situation."

Lindsey's expression softened, her understanding evident. "I know, Bella. It's a delicate situation, and you have to be careful. But sometimes life throws us a curve ball, and we adapt. Sometimes it's good. Sometimes not. Either way, it's up to you to decide what to do with it.

Her words resonated with me, reminding me that life is rarely black and white. Sometimes, we find ourselves in situations that challenge our beliefs and test our boundaries.

As Lindsey and I continued to talk, sharing our thoughts and fears, I felt a sense of relief wash over me.

Now that I had trusted advice from my best friend, I was ready to go even further, and dive into this exploration head first with Father Elijah. Whether it would remain purely sexual or turn into a relationship of sorts was still up in the air. But I was hopeful, nonetheless.

I sat in his office waiting for Father Elijah to finish up with confessions. I found myself utterly powerless as a flurry of vivid images invaded my thoughts, replaying the events that unfolded in the confessional just a few days prior.

Butterflies, the good kind, swirled in my tummy.

"Bella?"

CHAPTER 8

Elijah

I walk into the office to grab my things and go home for the day, only to find my little halo sitting on the edge of the chair in front of my desk wringing her hands. It appears to be a nervous gesture that I don't even think she realizes she's doing.

"Bella?" I say to get her attention. "This is a nice surprise."

"Umm… Hi, Father Elijah." She startles and greets me with a meek voice.

"What's going on? Something I can help you with?" I ask as I pull my chair out from behind my desk and sit across from her giving her my undivided attention.

"I was hoping to talk to you." She whispers as she looks up at me with her innocent gaze.

"Tell me what's wrong."

"I've been thinking and I was hoping that you would teach me more things. More than what you've already showed me."

I watch her intently as I decode her mannerisms. She appears shy, but I can see the mischievous glint in her eyes.

Bella's Father hasn't been in her life in a very long time,

and because her family is a part of my congregation, I guess I sort of took on a role as the only father figure in her life.

"Come here." I say as I pat my lap. She eyes it warily but does as I directed her to do. As she sits down sideways she wraps an arm around my neck and leans further into my embrace.

I turn my head speak softly against her ear. "You want to be daddy's little girl, Bella? Is that what you're asking?"

"Yes. I want you to teach me how to please you."

"How to please me or how to please a man? Because I assure you, those are two very different things. I'm grown, Bella. I've had years to develop particular tastes. I know my likes and dislikes. Are you willing to give me what I need? If so, I'll give you what you desire. I'll be your daddy and you can be my baby girl. But that means you do as I say. Can you do that?"

"Yes, daddy. Anything." She replies eagerly.

I feel a surge of power as Bella's words hang in the air. It's a delicate dance we're about to embark on, one that requires trust and understanding. I gently brush a strand of hair behind her ear, my touch lingering for a moment longer than necessary.

"Good girl," I whisper, my voice laced with a mix of authority and tenderness. "Remember, this dynamic is built on mutual respect and consent. I will guide you, protect you, and nurture you, but you must trust me completely."

Bella nods, her eyes filled with a mix of anticipation and vulnerability. I can sense her eagerness to explore this uncharted territory, to surrender herself to my guidance. It's a responsibility I don't take lightly.

"First and foremost, communication is key," I continue, my voice steady. "You must always feel comfortable expressing your desires, your limits, and your concerns. Daddy's little girl should never feel afraid to speak her mind."

Bella's grip tightens around my neck, her trust in me evident. I can't help but feel a swell of pride at her willingness to embark on this journey together. But I also know that trust must be earned and nurtured over time.

"Remember, Bella, this dynamic is not just about fulfilling my needs. It's about creating a safe space for you to explore your own desires and fantasies. I want to help you grow, to guide you towards your own pleasure and fulfillment."

She nods again, her eyes shining with a mix of excitement and vulnerability. I can see the hunger for knowledge in her gaze, the desire to learn and please. But I also know that this path we're treading is not without its challenges.

"There will be rules, boundaries, and expectations," I explain, my voice firm but gentle. "But always remember that your well-being and happiness are my utmost priority."

Bella's smile is radiant, a mix of trust and adoration. In that moment, I know that this arrangement will forever change us both.

I DECIDE TO INVITE BELLA TO MY HOME SINCE IT'S SO CLOSE TO the church. Turn down the gravel path next to the church and follow it back through the trees where you'll be met with a cozy two bedroom cabin. It's not much as far as space, but it's newly built with modern appliances and all the comforts of a regular home.

I set my keys on the counter, grab a couple bottles of water from the fridge, and then lead Bella to the bedroom.

"Take off your clothes." I instruct her.

"Yes, daddy." She says with a shaky breath.

I love hearing those words on her lips, but right now silence is the best thing for her.

She removes the thin spaghetti straps of her light pink, floral summer dress and it falls to the floor pooling at her feet.

I undo the white collar around my neck and unbutton my shirt. I remove it and toss it aside.

"Remove the rest. Don't be shy baby." I speak in a gentle voice to help sooth Bella's nerves.

I watch as she removes her white cotton bra and panties. Her breasts are perky, but no more than a handful, with small dusty rose colored nipples. They're perfect. The longer I look at them the more puckered they become. My little girl is getting turned on.

I step forward and palm her breasts. Leaning down I take her nipple into my mouth and run my tongue around it, feeling it stiffen even more.

I back away and remove what's left of my clothes. I hear her suck in a sharp breath. I'm sure this is the first time she's ever seen a dick in person before. I continue to stroke my cock slowly while I watch her, watch me.

She licks her lips and I know it's time.

"On your knees." I command in a firm but steady voice. Her eyes dart to mine and she does as she's told.

I step forward and rub the head of my weeping dick across her bottom lip.

"Lick your lips." I instruct.

Her eyes glance up at mine looking eager and hopeful.

"Be a good girl, baby, and lick and suck on my length like it's your very own lollipop. Can you do that for me?"

"Yes, daddy." She says breathily.

Learning forward she sticks out her tongue and slowly runs it up one side and down the other. She finds her way to the head and flicks her tongue back and forth over my slit, tasting my precum.

I let out a low groan, feeling a surge of desire coursing through my veins. Her obedience and eagerness only fuel my own arousal, and I can't help but tighten my grip on her hair, guiding her movements.

Her tongue continues its exploring, tracing every inch of my length with a delicate touch. Each flick and swirl sends shivers down my spine, intensifying the pleasure building within me. I watch her with a mix of admiration and hunger, captivated by the way she devotes herself to pleasing me.

As she reaches the sensitive tip, her lips part slightly, enveloping me in a warm, wet embrace. The sensation is exquisite, and I can't help but let out a throaty moan. Encouraged by my response, she begins to suck gently, her mouth creating a delicious suction that drives me wild.

"Look at you being such a good girl for daddy. That's it. Just like that."

I lose myself in the moment, my fingers tightening in her hair as she continues. Her tongue teasing and exploring, as she takes me deeper into her mouth.

I can feel my control slipping, the need to release becoming overwhelming. But I want to savor this moment, to prolong the pleasure as much as possible. So, with a gentle tug on her hair, I guide her to slow down, to tease me with a torturous rhythm that keeps me on the edge.

Her eyes meet mine. She understands my desire, my need for this sweet torment. And she willingly complies, her movements becoming even more deliberate, her lips and tongue working together.

Time seems to stand still as the intensity builds, the pleasure reaching its peak. With a final, desperate thrust, I can no longer hold back. I release with a guttural groan, my body trembling with ecstasy as she eagerly takes in every drop.

"Show me." I instruct quietly and she sticks out her tongue showing me her achievement. "Now swallow." I watch as her throat moves proving she's done as I asked. Before I get the chance to ask, my halo sticks out her tongue again to show me she's doing as she's told.

"Bed. Now." I say as I turn her around and give her a tap on the ass.

CHAPTER 9

Bella

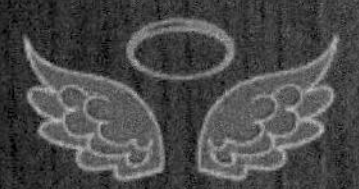

I crawl over the bed slipping under the comforter as I roll onto my back and I hear him chuckle behind me.

"Are you hiding from me?" Daddy asks.

I quickly kick the covers off of me exposing myself to him.

"Spread your legs."

I comply and before I know it he's gone. I should have known. Of course he wouldn't want an eighteen year old. He's too mature for me, too sexy.

"Are you on birth control?" He asks, starling me. When did he get back? He stands there holding a condom.

"No. Not yet. I didn't know exactly what we would be doing and it's hard to do things like that with my mom around." I say with regret lacing my words.

While the other night was life altering for me, just mentioning my mother to him makes me furious. Call it jealousy if you want. I'm perfectly fine admitting it. Not only that, but if he only knew how evil she truly was I'm not sure he would ever want to go near her again.

Maybe I should tell him after all.

"I have no desire to use this."

I bite my lip, weighing the consequences of not using protection.

"Then don't." I reply huskily.

He takes a deep breath as if he was holding it awaiting my response.

He looks at me and I can tell he's trying to process my words. I can't help but feel a surge of vulnerability, wondering if I've just crossed a line that we may not be ready for.

"Are you sure?" he asks softly, his voice filled with genuine concern. "I don't want to take any risks, especially if it's something you're not comfortable with."

"I'm sure." I reply.

He climbs onto the bed and as his body presses against mine, a sense of warmth and security washes over me. I can feel his heartbeat against my chest, steady and strong, matching the rhythm of my own.

His lips find mine, a tender and passionate kiss that ignites a fire within me. Our bodies meld together, skin against skin.

"This is going to hurt and you may bleed a bit. Are you sure you're ready for this?" He asks and I nod my head yes, unable to speak the words aloud right now, but he knows this.

"I'll take it slow and easy for your first time. But I'm telling you now Bella, each time after this will be much different. Hard. Rough."

He grabs my legs and wraps them up around his waist. My arms going around his neck once more. As he positions himself at my entrance, a mix of anticipation and nervousness courses through me.

With a gentle yet firm pressure, he begins to push forward, slowly breaching the barrier between us. I feel a slight discomfort, a stretching sensation that causes me to tense up momentarily. But his touch, his reassuring presence, helps me relax and surrender to the moment.

As he continues to inch forward, the discomfort gradually gives way to a mix of pleasure and sensation.

I let out a soft gasp as he fully enters me, our bodies becoming one. The feeling of fullness overwhelms me, a mix of pleasure and a hint of pain. But it's a pain that I willingly embrace.

"Fuck." He mutters under his breath.

He pauses, giving me a moment to adjust, to find my rhythm. I take a moment to savor the feeling of him inside me, the way our bodies fit together perfectly. And when I'm ready, I give him a subtle nod, a silent invitation to continue.

I wrap my legs tighter around his waist, pulling him closer, craving the intimacy that only he can provide.

As our bodies move in unison, the discomfort fades away, replaced by waves of pleasure. I lose myself in the sensations, in the way he fills me completely, in the way our bodies move together as if they were made for this very moment.

"So damn tight. Love the way this pussy wraps around my cock. You were made just for me." He says with his face buried into my neck.

His words send a shiver of desire down my spine, intensifying the pleasure that courses through me. I cling to him, my nails digging into his back, as he continues to thrust with a growing urgency.

"In the name of the father." he whispers.

The rhythm of our bodies becomes more primal, more instinctual. Each movement brings us closer to the edge, pushing us towards a shared release that promises to be explosive. I can feel the tension building within me, the coil of pleasure tightening with every thrust.

His lips find mine once again, a passionate and desperate kiss that mirrors the intensity of our connection. Our breaths mingle, our moans and gasps blending together.

"The son." He adds.

As the pleasure reaches its peak, I feel a surge of warmth spreading through me, radiating from the depths of my being. It's a wave of bliss that crashes over us. I can feel my womb fill with his warm seed. Spurt after spurt.

"And the holy ghost." He grunts out.

We cling to each other, our bodies trembling with the aftershocks of our shared release.

"Amen." We murmur together.

CHAPTER 10
Elijah

I stand at the pulpit giving a sermon on how god forgives. I know my Bella and if I had to guess, she's most likely spiraling right now over her indiscretions with me earlier in the week. But I'm certain that neither of us regret them. Nor do we truly seek forgiveness knowing that we're going to sin again and again.

Today Bella's wearing her powder blue dress again and with it being my favorite, it's hard for me to keep my eyes off of her.

As I continue speaking about God's forgiveness, I can't help but feel a mix of guilt and desire whenever my gaze falls upon Bella.

Her powder blue dress hugs her curves in all the right places, accentuating her beauty in a way that captivates my attention. The soft fabric dances with every movement she makes, and I find myself longing to reach out and touch it, to feel the warmth of her skin beneath my fingertips.

But I must resist these temptations in front of my flock, for I am a man of faith, standing before my congregation, preaching about the power of forgiveness.

Bella, too, seems aware of the tension that lingers between

us. Her eyes occasionally meet mine, and in those fleeting moments, I see a reflection of the same longing that resides within me. It is a silent understanding, a shared secret that binds us together in a web of forbidden passion.

Yet, as I continue to preach, I remind myself that forgiveness is not just for others but for ourselves as well. We are all flawed, prone to making mistakes and succumbing to our desires. It is in these moments of weakness that we must seek forgiveness, not only from a higher power but also from within.

I know that Bella and I may continue to sin, unable to resist the magnetic pull that draws us closer. But perhaps, in the depths of our transgressions, we can find solace in the knowledge that forgiveness is always within reach.

As the sermon comes to an end, I offer a final prayer for forgiveness, not only for myself but for all those who have strayed from the path of righteousness. And as I step down from the pulpit, I catch Bella's eye once more, silently vowing to make this woman mine in every sense of the word.

I can see Regina Thornfield dragging Bella through the crowd attempting to reach me faster as I see everyone off and shake hands at the door.

That woman truly is a snake in the grass. The things I know she's capable of weigh heavily on my mind every time I see either of them.

As I greet the congregation at the door, exchanging pleasantries and offering words of encouragement, I can sense Regina Thornfield's presence drawing nearer. Her piercing gaze and calculating smile send a shiver down my spine, reminding me of the darkness that lurks beneath her seemingly innocent facade.

I know all too well the lengths to which Regina is willing to go to achieve her desires. Her manipulative nature and cunning tactics have left a trail of broken hearts and shattered lives in her wake. Bella has become entangled in her web of deceit over the years.

The weight of this knowledge burdens my mind, casting a shadow over the joyous atmosphere of the church. I cannot help but worry for Bella's well-being, knowing that Regina's influence could lead her down a treacherous path. The thought of Bella being dragged through the crowd, under Regina's control, fills me with a sense of urgency and protectiveness.

But I must tread carefully, for exposing Regina's true nature could have dire consequences. She is a master of manipulation, capable of twisting the truth to suit her own agenda.

As I bid farewell to the last of the congregants, my mind races with thoughts of how to protect Bella from her mother's clutches.

But for now, I must put on a brave face, concealing my concerns behind a mask of serenity. As I watch Regina and Bella approach, I offer them a warm smile, masking the turmoil within. It is a battle of wills, a silent war fought in the depths of my soul, as I strive to protect Bella from the snake in the grass that is Regina Thornfield.

"Will we see you at the picnic this afternoon?" Regina asks once she reaches me.

"Yes, I'll be there," I respond to Regina's question, maintaining the facade of normalcy despite the unease that lingers within me.

As Regina finally releases my hand and steps aside, her presence still looms nearby, a constant reminder of her watchful eyes. It has become increasingly apparent that she is not only possessive of me but also jealous of her own daughter, Bella. The attention that Bella receives seems to ignite a fire of envy within Regina, fueling her manipulative tendencies.

I can't help but feel a pang of sympathy for Bella, caught

in the crossfire of her mother's insecurities. It is a toxic dynamic, one that threatens to suffocate the blossoming connection between Bella and me. The intimacy we share only serves to intensify Regina's jealousy, making her more determined to exert control over every aspect of Bella's life.

But I refuse to let Regina's toxic influence dictate our our happiness.

As the picnic approaches, I steel myself for the challenges that lie ahead. I know that Regina will be there, her eyes fixed on Bella and me, ready to pounce on any opportunity to assert her dominance. But I am determined to protect Bella, to shield her from the venomous grasp of her own mother.

With a deep breath, I prepare to face the afternoon, knowing that the battle has only just begun.

I walk around the church picnic mingling with those in attendance. Everyone wants to talk to the priest, unluckily for me. There are days when I love my calling and then there are days I just want to go home and shut my door, but my job is pretty hands on every hour of every day.

I catch site of my little girl out of the corner of my eye sitting with Lindsey and her family.

Lindsey and Bella have been inseparable since they were young, sharing secrets and experiences as best friends often do. It is only natural to assume that they have discussed the moments Bella and I have shared.

I approach Lindsey and her family, offering a warm smile as I join their conversation. It is important for me to maintain a sense of normalcy, to show Bella that our connection does not define who we are. I engage in light-hearted banter, asking about their day.

As the conversation continues, I steal glances at Bella, observing her interactions with Lindsey. She seems carefree, her laughter filling the air. It is a bittersweet sight, a reminder of the innocence that I strive to preserve in her young heart, even though I may have taken the innocence from her body.

It's with those thoughts that I find myself reflecting back on the afternoon we spent together in my bed as she gave her innocence to me. I could tell she had been in pain from me taking her virginity and she did bleed. However, she seems to be doing much better today.

I attempt willing my cock into submission before standing up, but now that the thoughts of Bella's sinful body are in my head, I know I won't feel relief until I've pleasured myself to the thought of my heaven sent little halo and her ethereal pussy.

I stand and make my way back inside the church as Bella watches on. She's probably wondering why I'm leaving them. If she only knew it was the memory of my length being sheathed inside her that was driving me mad.

I walk around the podium and slide behind the baptism pool where there's a corner that I know I can hide in while I stroke my length. It also gives me the perfect view of where my Bella sits every Sunday so I can imagine her just as she was in my dream only weeks ago. Sitting in the front pew, sliding her dress up and giving me a peek at what's underneath.

I press one palm against the wall while the other quickens the strokes as my fist chokes my hardened cock. The echoes of her moans and the taste of her lips linger in my mind, driving me to the edge of sanity.

As I stroke myself in the secluded corner, a mix of guilt and pleasure washes over me. The forbidden nature of my actions only adds fuel to the fire burning within. I can't help but imagine Bella's soft touch, her delicate hands exploring every inch of my body, igniting a fire that only she can extinguish.

I close my eyes and let my imagination run wild. I envision Bella's flushed cheeks and the way her eyes sparkle with desire. The thought of her surrendering herself to me, willingly succumbing to the pleasure.

"Daddy?" I stiffen as I hear the angelic voice coming from directly behind me.

CHAPTER 11
Bella

I stand here off to the side and watch Father Elijah touch himself hoping like hell that he's thinking of me. Just the thought of it is making me wet between my legs.

"Daddy?" I whisper in awe, not meaning to speak it out loud but unable to control myself. He stops abruptly then turns his head. He glances around the corner to see if anyone else is witnessing the sinful act in the house of the lord, but we're alone.

Father Elijah leans over gripping my wrist and pulls me towards him. He then turns me so that I'm against the wall and presses his lips to mine. I can feel his thick bulge press against me causing me to rub my legs together seeking friction that I know will only find when he deems it so.

"Fuck, Bella. I want you so damn bad, baby." He says with a raspy voice.

"Take me, daddy. Please." I beg.

He quickly undoes his pants, freeing his cock from the confines of his slacks, while I lift up my dress. He reaches down, tearing my light blue panties from my body. The cool air dancing upon my moistened slit.

"You shaved." He states not as a question but as a fact as a grin tugs at the corner of his mouth.

"I thought you'd like it." I reply.

"I do baby. I do. Daddy loves it."

He picks me up and I wrap my legs around his waist as he guides his thick ten inch shaft to my entrance.

He slowly enters my body and I feel a slight burning sensation as I stretch to accommodate his length.

"I love this pussy." He growls into my ear while thrusting forward once more.

"I love your cock, daddy." I quietly whimper.

The intimate act of shaving has heightened my senses, making every touch, every caress, feel more intense than before. The vulnerability of being completely bare, exposed to him, amplifies the connection we share.

As he moves closer, his presence engulfs me, and I can't help but gasp at the surge of desire that courses through my veins. The electricity between us crackles in the air.

With each thrust, I feel his length penetrating deeper, filling me completely. The sensation is overwhelming, a delicious mix of pleasure and aching need. Every nerve ending in my body is alive, responding to his every touch, his every movement.

Our moans and whispers fill the room, reminding us that we need to be quiet so we're not overheard.

Before I realize what's happening, we're moving, but I'm not sure where to. I can feel Father Elijah walking down steps and then I gasp for air as I feel my pussy being submerged in water as he continues to walk. It's not until this moment that I understand he's walked us straight into the baptism pool, clothes and all.

He then turns around and places me on the side of the pool and begins to thrust into me even harder.

"Tell me how much you love daddy's dick." He then reaches between us and begins to rub my bundle of nerves.

"I love it, daddy! So much." I reply.

"You know what daddy's doing? Baptizing this pussy. Making it born again. It's gonna weep for me isn't it little girl?"

I'm not only shocked by what's coming out of his mouth and how dirty it is, but I feel myself gush at how turned on it makes me.

"My little girl loves when daddy talks dirty to her." He says with a grunt as he thrusts back and forth inside me while continuing to rub my clit. "You want to come for daddy?"

"Yes! Please." I beg again.

"Squirt all over daddy baby. Baptize my cock in your cum so we can be reborn together." He rasps while he continues to impale me on his length, massaging my nub even faster than before.

I feel the heat spreading through my body and tingling setting in around my nerves.

"Oh fuck! I'm coming, daddy!" I nearly shout in ecstasy.

"That's it, baby. Keep going. Give it to me." He says as he continues to rub my sensitive bud even through my orgasm making it build again rapidly.

I dig my fingers into his hair, press my lips to his, and bite down while my moans grow louder until I feel myself explode and contract around him, milking his cock for all it's worth.

"Fuck!" He shouts as he empties his seed inside me.

I feel the pressure build in my canal and before I realize it, I'm doing just as he told me to do and baptizing his cock with my cum.

"Such a good girl. Look at that, baby. So proud of you." He coos at me while I continue to squirt and he pushes me back slightly so I can witness myself covering him in my juices for the first time.

A moment later and we're both breathing heavily, trying to catch our breath.

It's then that I realize we're both soaking wet, not only with our cum, but from the pool.

He must sense my panic. "If anyone says anything, you wanted to be born again and recommit your life to the lord. They don't have to know that you made that commitment to me instead." He reassures me with a smirk and I can't help the giggle that escapes me, causing him to laugh as well.

As the laughter subsides, we walk out of the pool and he takes a step closer, his eyes searching mine for any sign of doubt.

"You know we're in this together. Right?" He asks with sincerity.

"I know," I reply, "thank you."

It's nice to know we understand each other with little looks here, a gesture there. Even with our age difference, it's like this man, the man that's been there for me my entire life, is my soul mate.

He's introducing me to things I never would have expected, yet my body yearns for. His words. His touch. His sin.

And he's all mine. I'll make sure of it.

CHAPTER 12

Elijah

Bella went to the bathroom to clean up as best she can for a girl that just got fucked in a baptism pool filled with water, and I go to my office to change as well. When I come out I can hear Regina Thornfield down by the bathrooms yelling at Bella while dragging her down the hallway.

"You think you're so smart don't you? But you're not fooling me! You're evil, Isabella! Evil!" Regina says while stopping to point in Bella's face, then continues dragging her down the hallway.

"Let go of me mother!" Bella raises her voice at an attempt to get away from her.

My heart races and I grind my teeth as I witness the confrontation unfolding before me. Regina Thornfield, a woman known for her sharp tongue, fake niceties, and relentless pursuit of power, has Bella in her clutches. The fear in Bella's eyes is palpable, but there's also a flicker of defiance, a refusal to be broken by Regina's cruel words.

I want to make my way towards them and demand that she let her go as the anger simmers within me. But now isn't the time.

"You go out there and act like a good, wholesome, god-fearing young woman, with class. Something we both know you don't have. We'll finish this conversation at home after the picnic. You stay where I can see you. Don't anger me anymore than you already have, Isabella. I'll see you outside." Regina spits out and then leaves Bella standing alone in the hallway as she joins the picnic once again.

Bella turns around and tries to dodge me as I catch up to her.

"What the hell was that?" I ask angrily. I hope she knows I'm not angry at her but seeing her mother treat her that way pissed me off.

"Nothing. It was nothing." Bella quickly denies and then rushes to the doors to join the rest of the congregation outside.

CHAPTER 13

Bella

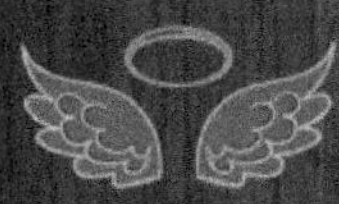

Mother makes me strip out of my clothes and stand in the shower. She grabs bleach and starts dousing my skin with it then throws a Brillo pad at me, "scrub yourself clean Isabella and pray that the lord forgives you of your sins, because I won't," She angrily exclaims.

I stand there, the stinging sensation intensifying as the bleach seeps into my open wounds from the lashings she gave me with the whip. The pain is unbearable, but I remain resolute, determined not to give her the satisfaction of seeing me break. I pick up the Brillo pad and begin to scrub my skin vigorously, desperately trying to rid myself of the burning chemicals.

As I scrub, I can't help but wonder how it has come to this. How did my mother, the person who is supposed to protect and love me, become so consumed by anger and hatred? The words she spews at me are like daggers, piercing through my already wounded soul. But I refuse to let her define me. I refuse to let her twisted version of love destroy my spirit.

The water cascades down my body, mixing with the tears streaming down my face. I close my eyes and silently pray for strength, for the courage to endure this torment. I pray for forgiveness, not from a vengeful deity, but from myself. For the guilt and shame that have been unjustly placed upon my shoulders.

I wish Father Elijah was here.

As the minutes stretch into what feels like an eternity, I can feel the burn subsiding, replaced by a numbness that spreads through my body. The physical pain may fade, but the emotional scars will remain, etched into my very being with the years of scars already occupying the space. Yet, I refuse to let them define me. I refuse to let this moment define my worth

With trembling hands, I turn off the shower and step out, my body still raw and tender. I wrap myself in a towel, my only shield against the world that seems so cruel and unforgiving.

Walking past my mother, I catch a glimpse of her reflection in the mirror. Her eyes, once filled with love so very long ago, now hold only bitterness and regret. In that moment, I realize that her actions are not a reflection of who I am, but rather a reflection of her own pain and brokenness.

With every step I take away from that bathroom, I am one step closer to reclaiming my own identity, one step closer to finding the love and acceptance I deserve, hopefully with Father Elijah by my side.

IT FEELS LIKE IT'S BEEN DAYS SINCE MOTHER LOCKED ME IN THIS room. It's in the same wing as my bedroom but further down

the hall and around a corner. You wouldn't even know it was there unless you walked all the way down.

There's a small cot with a thin sheet and and small pillow. The room has a toilet in the corner with no sink and no windows. I'm delivered bread and water once a day when I'm locked in this room.

The isolation in here is suffocating. The walls seem to close in on me. Time loses all meaning as I count the days by the meager meals that are slid through a small opening in the door to my cell. Because that's what this is, my very own prison designed by my mother disguised as Thornfield Manor on the outside, and hell within.

The bread is stale and tasteless. The water is lukewarm and barely quenches my thirst. It's a cruel existence, stripped of basic comforts and human dignity.

I close my eyes and imagine a world beyond these confines, a world where I am free and loved by Elijah. I hold onto that vision tightly.

I refuse to be defined or defeated by this room. I've had many trips here. But it has been a while since my last visit, months at least.

I think I've been here five days so far. It shouldn't be too much longer because people will start asking why I haven't been around, whether it be school or friends. But she already knows this and I'm sure she's already concocted and delivered the perfect excuse to appease everyone involved. She wouldn't dare tell them she caught her part time lover fuck her daughter in the baptism pool at our church.

I'VE BEEN ASLEEP, UNSURE OF HOW LONG I WAS OUT, BUT I WAKE up sweating with a pool of heat between my legs. I was having the most delicious dream and I refuse to let the only good thing that's come from this room drift away. So, I continue to fantasize and slip my hand inside my damp panties, feeling the moisture along my slit. I guide my other hand up and pinch my hardened nipple causing a moan to slip free.

I continue to tease my clit, rubbing it in a circular motion, swirling the wetness around. I'm so worked up. It's like Elijah popped the seal on my sexuality and now I'm a horny, worked up mess, all the time.

I start rubbing faster but it's just not the same without Elijah watching me or doing it for me. I just need more friction. Something to rub against me. But in this room I have limited resources. I sit up and look around to see if there's anything I might be able to use, and an idea comes to mind. It's not the best, but it just might work.

I take my pillow, fold it in half, and straddle it. I've never been on top before so maybe this could help me figure it out and I could make Elijah proud the next time I see him.

I lower my drenched pussy down onto the pillow and slightly rock back and forth once, then twice.

"Oh god." I whisper, my clit grinding back and forth on the fabric, finally getting the friction I so desperately need.

I can't help but close my eyes and imagine my Elijah beneath me and all the dirty words that would spill from his lips.

I rock swiftly back and forth. "Daddy, you feel so good," I say while breathing heavily, "I'm going to come. Please let me be a good girl and come for you, daddy." I half whisper and half moan while letting my imagination run wild.

The heat spreads and the tingles on my clit increase. I pick up my pace, grinding harder into the pillow, bath and forth and in a circular motion, when I suddenly feel myself tip over the edge. Light bursting behind my eyelids while imagining Elijah licking and sucking up all the juice that drips out of me.

I fall to the side and lay down on the bed, flipping by pillow over to put under my head with my chest heaving.

I should have saved my strength but I couldn't help myself. I couldn't go another night without my daddy, even if he was only a fantasy this time.

CHAPTER 14

Elijah

It's been almost two weeks since I last saw Bella. The last I heard from her she was arguing with her mother at the church picnic. I assumed I would see her the following Sunday at service, but Regina claimed Bella was sick and at home. I offered to bring some soup by the manor but she declined, which is unusual for Regina Thornfield. Usually she looks for any excuse for me to stop by so I'm sure something is going on, I'm just not sure what.

I hear a knock at the door and glance at the time on my phone. It's eight o'clock in the evening and I'm not expecting company.

I open the door to find Bella looking back at me.

"It's good to see you up and about, baby. You had me worried. Your mom said you've been sick."

As I pulled Bella into a hug, I feel her body tense up, and she sucked in a quick breath. Concern flooded my senses, and I gently released her, my eyes scanning her face for any signs of discomfort or pain.

"Bella, what's wrong? Are you in pain?" I asked, my voice filled with worry.

She hesitated for a moment, her eyes avoiding mine. "It's

not just physical pain," she finally admitted, her voice barely above a whisper. "There's something else going on, something I can't fully explain right now."

My heart sank even further, but I knew I had to be patient and give her the space to open up at her own pace.

"Take your time, Bella. I'm here for you, no matter what it is," I reassured her, my voice filled with sincerity.

She took a deep breath, gathering her thoughts before speaking. "It's my mother," she began, her voice trembling. "We've always had our differences, but lately, it's been unbearable. She's been controlling every aspect of my life, suffocating me with her expectations and demands."

I listened intently, my heart breaking for Bella. I had always known that her relationship with her mother was complicated, as was mine, but I never realized the extent of the pain she was enduring.

"She saw us in the pool." She says, staring at the floor as if I would be upset with her or ashamed. I would never be embarrassed or regret anything we've done together.

"Well too bad for her, you're eighteen now. You don't have to put up with her antics anymore."

I reached out and gently lifted Bella's chin, ensuring that she met my gaze. "Bella, you have nothing to be ashamed of. Our connection, our love, it's something beautiful, and no one should make you feel otherwise," I said firmly, my voice filled with conviction.

She looked up at me, her eyes filled with a mix of relief and vulnerability. "I've always felt trapped by her judgments, her expectations. But you're right, I am eighteen now, and I deserve to live my life authentically."

"You do. I'm glad you realize that." I reply, proud that she's willing to finally standup for herself. "Now show me where it hurts so I can help you baby."

She stands and I follow her to my bedroom, happy that she felt comfortable enough to make herself feel at home. She removed her shirt she turns around and all of my good sense goes down the fucking drain.

"I'll kill her." I say as I grit my teeth, trying to not let my mouth get me in trouble.

"Please don't. She's not worth it." Bella says with distress in her voice. I reassure her it was only a figure of speech, even though I'm not sure if that was a lie or not just yet.

She goes on to explain everything that's happened and I feel like an asshole for sleeping with her evil bitch of a mother for so long, and for not paying more attention to Bella over the years.

"She thinks I'm staying at Lindsey's tonight." She whispers. I detect a hint of hope in her voice and flash a smile in her direction as I lead her to the shower.

"Good. You'll stay here then."

We get to the bathroom and she slowly removes her clothes, afraid to show me her wounds. I'm not sure if she's embarrassed or afraid of what I might do to the woman that's caused her so much pain over the years.

As she turns I take in the welts and bruises. There's a few places with open wounds but not as deep as I was imagining, so she won't have to worry about any scarring. Not for my sake but for hers. I can't imagine what a physical reminder of this time in her life would cause to her mental stability. Although, if anything, she's proven how strong she is to have survived all of this on her own for so long.

She gets in the shower and wets her hair. I step in behind her and squirt shampoo into the palm of my hands and begin massaging her scalp and lathering her hair. I hear her hum in pleasure over the sound of the water hitting the shower floor.

"This is bliss." She coos as I lean down and plant a kiss on the base of her neck.

"Good. I'm glad you're enjoying it." I reply, "Let's get this rinsed out and lather in some conditioner."

After rinsing the conditioner I decide to make her feel

good in other ways as I detach the nozzle from the shower wall.

"What are you doing?" She asks curiously.

"Taking care of my little girl." I reply and earn the sweet smile I was hoping for.

I wrap my arms around her and pull her back gently into my front. I lower my right hand that's holding the shower nozzle and turn the jets up to a pulsating speed, pressing it against her clit.

She squeaks in surprise and immediately starts breathing heavily.

"What..what are you doing?" She asks.

"I already told you. Taking care of my little girl. Relax and let daddy take care of you."

CHAPTER 15
Bella

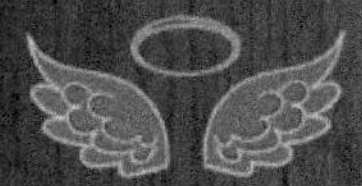

I feel the water pulsating against my pussy and immediately feel close to going over the edge.

"How…how are you doing that?" I ask and hear my question of amazement followed by a small chuckle in my ear.

"I'm not doing it, the water is. It feels good. Doesn't it?" He asks, and I nod my head yes. "Mhmm." I manage to mumble out.

He begins pressing the nozzle harder against my clit and I feel it massaging me with even more pressure. Before I know it my legs are shaking and I tip over the edge in record time.

"There you go. Good girl." He murmurs in my ear.

We finish washing each other and then head to the bedroom and climb into bed as if this is our regular routine. It feels so normal. Like we do this every day.

He cuddles up behind me and I press my ass into his length, unable to stay away.

"You really don't want to do that." He whispers in my ear.

"Why not?" I ask curious as to why he wouldn't want to be with me again.

"You want me to fuck your ass right now?" He asks and I hop up and face him.

"Do what?!" I screech in disbelief, which only amuses him further.

"I'm kidding," he says with a laugh, "we can try that another time. Right now I want you on all fours. Ass up."

I follow his command and turn around with curious eyes. "Now what?" I ask, genuinely curious.

He slides in behind me stroking his cock then settles it against my entrance, and slams his rod into my canal. I scream from the pain but it soon turns to pleasure as I feel his thick cock knocking against my cervix, stretching me over and over again.

I feel a tug on my hair as he grips my long blonde hair and twists it around his arm to get a better grip and more traction.

"You like taking daddy's dick little girl?" He pants.

"Yes, daddy!" I moan out in response.

"I love this tight little pussy." He says as he slaps my ass hard enough for the sound to echo throughout the room.

I don't think I've ever felt anything as good as this. The pain mixed with pleasure is calling out to me. He warned me the first time that it would be the only time he would go easy on me and as much as I loved our first time together, I'm discovering that I prefer it hard and rough.

"Daddy's gonna put a baby in his little girl. You'd like that wouldn't you?" He grunts out. The sound of our skin slapping together is echoing off the walls of the bedroom.

"Fuck your seed deep inside me daddy! Please! I need it!" I scream out in reply as I feel my whole existence begin to shatter. Only seconds go by before I explode all over his cock, drenching the sheets as he fills me up with ropes of his hot, thick cum.

I WAKE UP TO MY PHONE RINGING. NO MATTER HOW MANY TIMES I don't answer it, it just starts ringing again. I snuggle into the covers intending to go back to sleep until I hear Elijah answer my phone, which has my eyes flying open because I'm almost certain it's my mother that's been blowing up my cell.

"She's asleep." He says quietly followed by a long pause.

"You can threaten me all you want, *Regina*, but Bella is no longer your concern." He continues, "You may be her mother, but soon I'll be her husband. So get over yourself. We'll be by later today to get her belongings."

I can't help the giggle that erupts from me as he's ending the call. It's only then he realizes that I've been awake and listening and he looks slightly flustered. Probably because of the husband comment, but *swoon*. I sigh like the horny love obsessed teenager that I am and he finally chuckles at my lovesick demeanor.

"I meant that, you know?" He says.

"Meant what?" I ask.

"That I'll soon be your husband."

"Good." I reply. He reaches over and tucks a strand of my long golden hair behind my ear and kisses me gently on the lips.

"I love you my little halo." He says sweetly, and I can't help but smile up at him. "I love you, too, daddy." I reply and he gives me a heartfelt smile in return.

As cheesy as it sounds, he's become my whole world in a matter of weeks. I've honestly loved him for years, but tried to pass it off as my first crush. He's been my only crush.

I know it won't be easy. With his position in the church and us having so many years difference between us, but I no longer care. He's everything to me, come what may.

CHAPTER 16

Elijah

As we drive closer to Thornfield Manor, I can see the anxiety etched on Bella's face. Her fingers fidget with the hem of her dress, and her eyes dart nervously out the window. I reach out and gently squeeze her hand, trying to offer some reassurance.

"Bella, everything will be alright," I say, my voice filled with conviction.

Bella's grip tightens around mine, and she manages a weak smile. "I know, but it's just... she's always been so controlling. I can't help but worry about how she'll react to us being together."

I nod, understanding the weight of her words.

We finally approach the grand gates of Thornfield Manor. The sprawling estate stands as a symbol of Bella's past.

Stepping out of the car, Bella takes a deep breath, steeling herself for what's to come. I wrap my arm around her, offering my unwavering support. Together, we walk towards the imposing front doors, ready to confront whatever challenges await us.

Inside, the air is heavy with tension. Bella's mother, Mrs. Thornfield, stands at the top of the grand staircase, her eyes cold and calculating. She surveys us with a critical gaze, her disapproval evident in every line of her face.

Bella takes a step forward, her voice steady but filled with emotion.

"Mother, I understand that you may not approve of our relationship, but we love each other. We deserve a chance to be happy."

Mrs. Thornfield's expression remains unchanged, her silence deafening. For a moment, doubt creeps into Bella's eyes, but I squeeze her hand, silently urging her to stay strong.

Finally, after what feels like an eternity, Regina speaks, her voice laced with icy disdain. "Love? You think this is love? It's nothing more than a foolish infatuation, Bella. You're throwing away everything I've worked for, everything I've built for you."

Bella's determination remains unshaken. "Mother, I refuse to sacrifice my own happiness for the sake of your expectations."

Mrs. Thornfield's face contorts with anger, her voice rising. "You ungrateful child! How dare you defy me? I will not allow this disgrace to tarnish our family's name."

But Bella stands her ground, her voice unwavering. "Mother, how can you stand there and honestly spout such things after all you've done? You manipulate and you lie. You abuse your own child physically and emotionally. You yourself slept with Father Elijah, not for love, but for lust. But the icing on the unholy cake, is that you did indeed murder my father and bury him in the garden out back." She says with a smirk on her face and mischief dancing in her eyes. "Secrets, secrets, are no fun." Bella says, scolding her mother.

"Do you honestly think I could grow up with you of all people and not be able to put the pieces of a conspiracy together?" She added, "The only way you would see even a penny of father's money was if no one knew he was dead. I guess that's what happens when there's a prenuptial agreement in place. Then poor Elijah here sleeps with you one time, and you blackmail him for years, threatening his standing in the church."

"You ungrateful little leech! I should have just put you in the ground with your father when I had the chance!" Regina screams as she hastily makes her way down the stairs.

The atmosphere in Thornfield Manor turns volatile as Bella's mother, Regina, unleashes her pent-up anger. Her face contorts with rage, her words dripping with venom. Bella's eyes widen in shock, but she refuses to back down.

Regina's face turns a shade of crimson, her fists clenched tightly. "You think you're so clever, don't you? Well, let me tell you something, Bella. Your father's money was rightfully mine, and I did what I had to do to secure it."

Regina's eyes dart between Bella and myself, her anger giving way to a flicker of fear. She realizes that her carefully constructed web of lies is beginning to unravel, and her grip on control is slipping away.

In a fit of rage, Regina lunges towards Bella, her hands outstretched as if to strangle her. But before she can reach her, I step in, blocking her path. "That's enough, Regina! You will not lay a hand on Bella."

Regina's face contorts with fury, her voice filled with venom. "You think you can protect her? You're nothing but a worthless outsider, a nobody!"

"I may not come from the same background as you, but I love Bella with all my heart. And I will do whatever it takes to keep her safe from your toxic influence."

Regina's eyes narrow, her breathing heavy with anger. "You will regret this, both of you. I will make sure of it." She then turns and goes after Bella again on the other side of me.

I didn't even see it coming.

Regina slips past me, grabbing onto Bella. She then slaps

her, digging her nails into her skin. Bella pushes her away in self-defense.

It all happens in slow motion. Regina falls backwards cracking her head on the bottom step of the grand staircase. Instantly, her head is surrounded in a pool of her own blood.

Bella and I both just stand there in shock.

"I'm going to prison. Aren't I? Did I do this?" She asks frantically.

I pull her to me stealing my arms around her, hurting her face in my chest while I kiss the top of her head and stroke her hair. "Shhh…it's okay baby. You didn't do anything wrong. She attacked you. It's self-defense." I reassure her while she begins to quietly sob into my shirt.

"This is true Mrs. Bella." Says a small voice from across the room. "I have proof," she says while holding up her cellphone.

Thank fuck. It looks like Regina didn't make any friends among her staff while she was still breathing. Luckily for us.

Bella and I turn our attention towards the source of the voice, surprised to see one of the staff members, Gracie, stepping forward with her cellphone in hand. Relief washes over us as we realize that we may have an unexpected ally in this chaotic situation.

Emily approaches us cautiously, her eyes filled with a mix of sympathy and determination. "I've been working for Mrs. Thornfield, Regina, for years, and I've seen the way she operates. I couldn't stand by and watch her hurt you anymore, Bella."

She shows us the screen of her cellphone, revealing a video recording of the entire altercation between us and Regina. It captures the moment when Regina lunged towards Bella, clearly displaying her aggressive intent.

"This video proves that it was self-defense," Gracie explains, her voice filled with conviction. "I'm willing to testify and provide any other evidence needed."

Bella's sobs begin to subside as hope flickers in her eyes. She looks up at Gracie, gratitude evident in her gaze. "Thank you, Gracie. Your support means the world to us."

Gracie nods, a small smile forming on her lips. "You deserve to be free."

With Gracie's evidence, there should be no legal problems.

I step aside and make the call to the police department.

Regina's reign of manipulation and deceit has come to an end, and Bella will finally be free to live her life as she sees fit. Hopefully as my wife, if she'll have me.

Epilogue

BELLA

TEN MONTHS LATER

Months have passed since that fateful day at Thornfield Manor.

The weight of my mother's absence lifted from my shoulders, and I finally felt free. Free from her control, free from her toxic influence. It was a bittersweet victory, knowing that my own mother had betrayed me in such a way, but it also allowed me to fully embrace the love and happiness that had been waiting for me all along.

With each passing day, I grew stronger, healing from the wounds inflicted by years of manipulation. Elijah stood by my side, his unwavering support and love guiding me through the darkest moments. Together, we rebuilt our lives, creating a future filled with trust, honesty, and genuine happiness.

Thornfield Manor, once a symbol of pain and secrets, became a place of healing and transformation. I no longer wanted to live in the property, but we found a good use for it. We renovated the estate, turning it into a sanctuary for those seeking refuge from their own pasts. It became a haven for survivors, a place where they could find solace and support from our church.

"ARE YOU SURE YOU WANT TO GO THROUGH WITH THIS? IT'S okay if you don't want to baby. I respect your decisions." Elijah said as we stood inside the church.

"We're doing this. You've waited long enough." I replied while patting Elijah's chest. "Besides, Lindsey has the twins for the day. So we better milk it for all its worth."

We both laughed and walked down the isle together, hand in hand. Once we were on the pulpit standing in front of the podium facing the pews, I leaned over while Eli flipped my dress over my waist, followed by three rapid slaps to my ass. He pulled himself from his pants and whispered in my ear, "You ready baby?"

"Yes, daddy." I replied excitedly. It was then that he thrust forward, sinking his cock deep inside my channel.

"Let us pray." He instructed, and so I did.

"Fuck me harder daddy," I begged and then continued, "forgive me father, for I have sinned…Oh, God. Yes!" I yelled as he hit just the right spot.

"Good girl."

THE END

Acknowledgments

To my husband. Thank you for always supporting me no matter how crazy I get. You the real MVP. Love you.

To my son, who better not have his eyes anywhere near these pages. It makes my heart happy every time you cheer me on, and you cheer me on every single day no matter what I'm doing. Lol Love you, bub.

Tash with Dazed Designs. Thank you for the sinful cover and putting up with my forgetful procrastinating ass.

Unalive Promotions for the book tours and formatting. You're pretty fucking cool. I wonder why? *wink*

To my Cult of Chaos ARC & Street Team, thank you for hanging in there while we get everything situated. This release has been insane, but you rocked it! Thank you for loving my books as much as I do.

To my Crimson Queens, and all the readers, bookstagrammers, booktokers, bloggers. Thank you so much for just being you. Your encouragement and support is everything to me. And as always, thank you for sharing, reading, reviewing, yelling, and screaming about my books to anyone who will listen. I love you all.

About the Author

Tristina Brockway is an enigmatic wordsmith who delves fearlessly into the realms of Dark Romance. Formerly a connoisseur of tequila, she's traded shots for pages, finding solace and inspiration within the world of books.

As a wife and devoted mother, her world revolves around her loving husband and her son, who is truly her universe. When not weaving intricate narratives, she's a dedicated animal lover, sharing her world with two feline companions, Oreo and Trix.

Beneath her dark and twisted sense of humor lies a writer who thrives in the comfort of her pajamas, often preferring their company over bustling crowds.
Embracing chaos as her muse, Tristina Brockway brings a captivating and unconventional perspective to the world of literature.

www.tristinabrockway.com

www.instagram.com/authortristinabrockway

www.tiktok.com/@authortristinabrockway

linktr.ee/authortristinabrockway